The Dinosaur Who Lived In My Backyard

B.G. HENNESSY   Pictures by SUSAN DAVIS

PUFFIN BOOKS

PUFFIN BOOKS
Published by the Penguin Group
A division of Penguin Books USA Inc.,
375 Hudson Street, New York, New York 10014, U.S.A.
Penguin Books Ltd, 27 Wrights Lane, London W8 5TZ, England
Penguin Books Australia Ltd, Ringwood, Victoria, Australia
Penguin Books Canada Ltd, 10 Alcorn Avenue, Toronto, Ontario, Canada M4V 3B2
Penguin Books (N.Z.) Ltd, 182-190 Wairau Road, Auckland 10, New Zealand

Penguin Books Ltd, Registered Offices: Harmondsworth, Middlesex, England

First published in the United States of America by Viking Penguin,
a division of Penguin Books USA Inc., 1988
Published in Picture Puffins, 1990
13 15 17 19 20 18 16 14
Text copyright © B.G. Hennessy, 1988
Illustrations copyright © Susan Davis, 1988
All rights reserved

LIBRARY OF CONGRESS CATALOGING IN PUBLICATION DATA
Hennessy, B. G. (Barbara G.)   The dinosaur who lived in my backyard / B.G. Hennessy ;
pictures by Susan Davis.   p.   cm.
Summary: A young boy imagines what it was like long ago when a dinosaur lived in his backyard.
ISBN 0-14-050736-1
[1. Dinosaurs—Fiction.]   I. Davis, Susan, 1948— ill.   II. Title.
[PZ7.H3914Di 1990]   [E]—dc20   89-36029

Printed in the United States of America
Set in Garamond #3

*For Matthew
and every other child
who has wished for a dinosaur of their own.*
B.G.H.

*For Jake
who taught me about dinosaurs
when he was four year old,
and for Jessica, John and Fes.
With love.*
S.D.

There used to be a dinosaur who lived in my backyard.
Sometimes I wish he still lived here.

The dinosaur who lived here
hatched from an egg that was
as big as a basketball.

By the time he was five, he was as big as our car.

Just one of his dinosaur feet
was so big it wouldn't even have
fit in my sandbox.

My mother says that if you eat all your vegetables you'll grow
very strong. That must be true, because that's all this dinosaur ate.
I bet he ate a hundred pounds of vegetables every day.
That's a whole lot of lima beans.

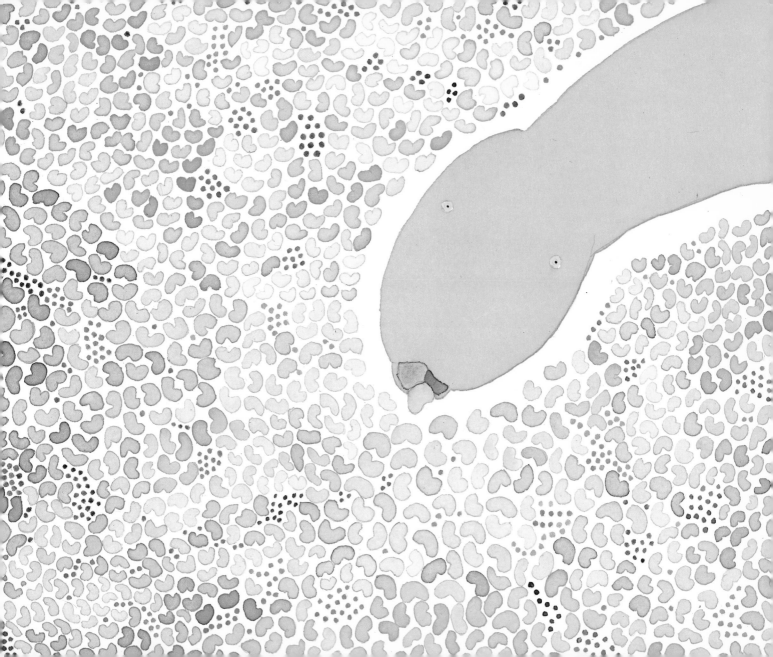

This dinosaur was so heavy that he would have made my whole neighborhood shake like pudding if he jumped. He weighed as much as twenty pick-up trucks.

The dinosaur who lived in my backyard
was bigger than my school-bus.
Even bigger than my house.

He had many other dinosaur friends.

Sometimes they played
hide-and-seek.

Sometimes they had terrible fights.

The dinosaur who used to live here was
allowed to sleep outside every night.
It's a good thing he didn't need a tent.
He was so big he would have needed a
circus tent to keep him covered.

Back when my dinosaur lived here,
my town was a big swamp.
This dinosaur needed a lot of water.
If he still lived here we'd have to keep
the sprinkler on all the time.

My dinosaur had a very long neck so he
could eat the leaves at the top of trees.
If he still lived here, I bet he
could rescue my kite.

That's all I know about the dinosaur who used to live in my backyard.

He hasn't been around
for a very long time.
Sometimes I wish he
still lived here.

It would be pretty hard to keep a dinosaur happy.
But my sister and I are saving all our lima beans—
just in case.